THE ADVENTURE ... 'ER

by **MARK TWAIN**

#6 Tom's Treasure Hunt

Adapted by Catherine Nichols

Illustrated by Nonna Aleshina

STERLING

New York / London
www.sterlingpublishing.com/kids

STERLING and the distinctive Sterling logo are
registered trademarks of Sterling Publishing Co., Inc.

Library of Congress Cataloging-in-Publication Data Available

Lot #: 10 9 8 7 6 5 4 3 2 1
02/10
Published by Sterling Publishing Co., Inc.
387 Park Avenue South, New York, NY 10016
© 2010 by Sterling Publishing Co., Inc
Illustrations © 2010 by Nonna Aleshina
Distributed in Canada by Sterling Publishing
^{c}/o Canadian Manda Group, 165 Dufferin Street
Toronto, Ontario, Canada M6K 3H6
Distributed in the United Kingdom by GMC Distribution Services
Castle Place, 166 High Street, Lewes, East Sussex, England BN7 1XU
Distributed in Australia by Capricorn Link (Australia) Pty. Ltd.
P.O. Box 704, Windsor, NSW 2756, Australia

Sterling ISBN 978-1-4027-6754-8

For information about custom editions, special sales, premium and
corporate purchases, please contact Sterling Special Sales
Department at 800-805-5489 or specialsales@sterlingpublishing.com.

Contents

Pirate Pals

Tom Sawyer ran outside.
It was the first day
of summer vacation.
He was ready for an adventure.
But what was there to do?

He could climb a tree.

Or go fishing.

Or swim in the watering hole.

They all were fun.

But Tom wanted to

do something new.

Tom saw Joe Harper and Huck Finn
coming down the road.
He waved to his friends.
"Where are you going?" Tom asked.
"Nowhere," Joe said.
"Just walking," Huck said.
Tom joined them.

The boys walked to the river.

Tom tossed a pebble into the water.

"School is out for the summer," he said.

We should be doing something special."

"Like what?" Joe asked.

In the river was a small island.

Pirates had stayed there long ago.

"Let's row to Pirate Island," Tom said.

"What could we do there?" Huck asked.

"Be pirates!" Tom said.

"And have adventures!"

On a Treasure Hunt

The boys packed for their trip.

Then they got on Tom's raft.

Tom gave the orders.

Joe and Huck paddled.

"Steady," Tom called out.
"Not too fast and
not too slow."
"Yes, sir!" Huck and Joe replied.

At last they landed
on Pirate Island.
Huck and Joe wanted to sleep.

"Don't sleep," Tom said.

"We're pirates, remember?"

"You just shouted orders," Huck said.

"We did all the work!"

Tom looked at his sleepy friends.

"I heard treasure is hidden

on the island," he told them.

Both boys sat up.

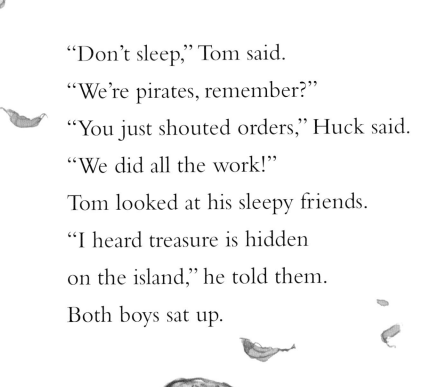

"Do you think we can find it?" Joe asked.

"Not if we don't look," Tom said.

"Let's go!" Huck said.

"I'll lead the way," Tom said.

A Dark Cave

Tom and his friends walked
all over the island.
But they didn't find the treasure.
"We've looked everywhere," Tom said.

Huck pointed to a cave.

"We haven't gone in there," he said.

The cave looked spooky.

Tom didn't want to go inside.

But he didn't want his friends

to think he was afraid.

He marched up to the cave.

Huck and Joe followed.

The boys lit candles
and went inside the dark cave.
Tom walked along
a narrow path.
His candle made shadows
on the walls.
Tom's knees shook.

The path ended.

Tom stepped into a big room.

Bats flew at him.

"Huck! Joe!"

Tom called for his friends.

No one answered.

Where were they?

Just then Tom's candle went out.

Treasure At Last!

Tom stood still.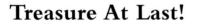

He couldn't see the bats.

But he could hear their squeaks.

Tom yelled for his friends again.

"We're over here!"

Huck and Joe yelled.

Tom followed their voices.

Soon Tom saw candlelight.

He ran toward his friends

and tripped over a large rock.

"Ouch!" Tom cried out.

Huck and Joe rushed over.

"I'm okay," Tom told them.

A mark was scratched on the rock.

Tom looked closer.

The mark was a big *X*.

"Why is that X there?" Joe asked.

"To show where treasure is buried,"
Tom said.

The three boys pushed the rock aside.

Underneath was a deep hole.

Tom put his hand in
as far as it could go.
His fingers touched wood.
He pulled out a small chest.
"Pirate treasure!" he whispered.

Tom opened the chest.

It was filled with gold coins.

"We're rich!" he shouted.

Tom looked at all the coins.

"What will Aunt Polly say

when I show her our treasure?" he said.

"She'll raise your
allowance for sure," Joe said.
"I bet we'll each get a
dollar a week," Huck said.
"Think of the fun we can have
with that much money," Tom said.

Tom filled his pockets
with the coins.
Only this morning he had wished
for an adventure.
His wish had really come true!